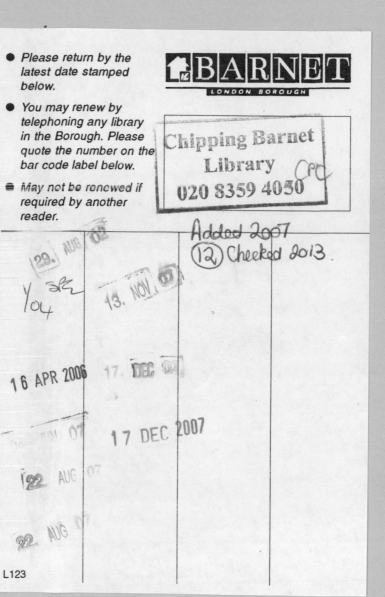

RAGGED BEAR'S BOOK OF

Nursery Rhymes

For Phoebe in her windy house
Diz

First published in the United Kingdom in 2001 by Ragged Bears Publishing Limited,
Milborne Wick, Sherborne, Dorset DT9 4PW

Distributed by Ragged Bears Limited, Ragged Appleshaw, Andover, Hampshire SP11 9HX
Tel: 01264 772269

Illustration copyright © 2001 by Diz Wallis

The right of Diz Wallis to be identified as illustrator of this work has been asserted

ALL RIGHTS RESERVED

A CIP record of this book is available from the British Library

ISBN 1 85714 221 7

Printed in China

RAGGED BEAR'S BOOK OF
Nursery Rhymes

100 NURSERY RHYMES SELECTED
AND ILLUSTRATED BY
Diz Wallis

Contents

Hey Diddle, Diddle

Hey diddle, diddle,
The cat and the fiddle,
The cow jumped over the moon;
The little dog laughed
To see such fun,
And the dish ran away with the spoon.

The Mischievous Raven

A farmer went trotting upon his grey mare,
Bumpety, bumpety, bump!
With his daughter behind him so rosy and fair,
Lumpety, lumpety, lump!

A raven cried, Croak! and they all tumbled down,
Bumpety, bumpety, bump!
The mare broke her knees and the farmer his crown,
Lumpety, lumpety, lump!

The mischievous raven flew laughing away,
Bumpety, bumpety, bump!
And vowed he would serve them the same the next day,
Lumpety, lumpety, lump!

Little Boy Blue

Little Boy Blue,
Come blow up your horn,
The sheep's in the meadow,
The cow's in the corn.
Where is the boy
Who looks after the sheep?
He's under a haycock
Fast asleep.
Will you wake him?
No, not I,
For if I do,
He's sure to cry.

Little Miss Muffet

Little Miss Muffet
Sat on a tuffet,
Eating her curds and whey;
There came a big spider,
Who sat down beside her
And frightened Miss Muffet away.

Pussy Cat, Pussy Cat

Pussy cat, pussy cat,
Where have you been?
I've been up to London
To look at the Queen.

Pussy cat, pussy cat,
What did you there?
I frightened a little mouse
Under her chair.

Peter, Peter, Pumpkin Eater

Peter, Peter, pumpkin eater,
Had a wife but couldn't keep her;
He put her in a pumpkin shell
And there he kept her very well.

Peter, Peter, pumpkin eater,
Had another, and didn't love her;
Peter learned to read and spell,
And then he loved her very well.

Up the Wooden Stairs to Bedfordshire

Up the wooden stairs to Bedfordshire,
Down Sheet Lane to Blanket Fair.

Come, Let's to Bed

Come, let's to bed,
Says Sleepy-head;
Tarry a while says Slow;
Put on the pan,
Says Greedy Nan,
Let's sup before we go.

Lavender's Blue, Diddle, Diddle

Lavender's blue, diddle, diddle,
Lavender's green;
When I am king, diddle, diddle,
You shall be queen.

Call up your men, diddle, diddle,
Set them to work,
Some to the plough, diddle, diddle,
Some to the cart.

Some to make hay, diddle, diddle,
Some to thresh corn,
While you and I, diddle, diddle,
Keep ourselves warm.

Simple Simon Met a Pieman

Simple Simon met a pieman,
Going to the fair;
Said Simple Simon to the pieman,
Let me taste your ware.

Says the pieman to Simple Simon,
Show me first your penny;
Says Simple Simon to the pieman,
Sir, I have not any.

Simple Simon went a-fishing
For to catch a whale;
All the water he had got
Was in his mother's pail.

Simple Simon went to look
If plums grew on a thistle;
He pricked his finger very much,
Which made poor Simon whistle.

Rub-a-Dub-Dub

Rub-a-dub-dub,
Three men in a tub,
And who do you think they be?
The butcher, the baker,
The candlestick-maker.
Turn 'em out, knaves all three.

Hush-a-Bye, Baby

Hush-a-bye, baby, on a tree top,
When the wind blows the cradle will rock;
When the bow breaks the cradle will fall,
Down will come baby, cradle and all.

This is the House That Jack Built

This is the house
that Jack built.

This is the malt
That lay in the house
that Jack built.

This is the rat,
That ate the malt
That lay in the house
that Jack built.

This is the cat,
That killed the rat,
That ate the malt
That lay in the house
that Jack built.

This is the dog,
That worried the cat,
That killed the rat,
That ate the malt
That lay in the house
that Jack built.

This is the cow with the
crumpled horn,
That tossed the dog,
That worried the cat,
That killed the rat,
That ate the malt
That lay in the house
that Jack built.

This is the maiden all forlorn,
That milked the cow with the crumpled horn,
That tossed the dog,
That worried the cat,
That killed the rat,
That ate the malt
That lay in the house
that Jack built.

This is the man all tattered and torn,
That kissed the maiden all forlorn,
That milked the cow with the crumpled horn,
That tossed the dog,
That worried the cat,
That killed the rat,
That ate the malt
That lay in the house
that Jack built.

This is the priest all shaven and shorn,
That married the man all tattered and torn,
That kissed the maiden all forlorn,
That milked the cow with the crumpled horn,
That tossed the dog,
That worried the cat,
That killed the rat,
That ate the malt
That lay in the house
that Jack built.

This is the cock that crowed in the morn,
That waked the priest all shaven and shorn,
That married the man all tattered and torn,
That kissed the maiden all forlorn,
That milked the cow with the
crumpled horn,
That tossed the dog,
That worried the cat,
That killed the rat,
That ate the malt
That lay in the house
that Jack built.

This is the farmer sowing his corn,
That kept the cock that crowed
in the morn,
That waked the priest all shaven
and shorn,
That married the man all
tattered and torn,
That kissed the maiden all forlorn,
That milked the cow with the
crumpled horn,
That tossed the dog,
That worried the cat,
That killed the rat,
That ate the malt
That lay in the house
that Jack built.

Cross-Patch

Cross-patch,
Draw the latch,
Sit by the fire and spin;
Take a cup,
And drink it up,
Then call your neighbours in.

Remember, Remember, the 5th of November

Remember, remember,
The 5th of November;
The gunpowder, treason and plot;
I see no reason
Why gunpowder treason
Should ever be forgot.

The Cock Doth Crow

The cock doth crow
To let you know
If you be wise
'Tis time to rise:
For early to bed,
And early to rise,
Is the way to be healthy
And wealthy and wise.

The North Wind Doth Blow

The north wind doth blow,
And we shall have snow,
And what will poor Robin do then?
Poor thing.
He'll sit in the barn,
And keep himself warm,
And hide his head under his wing,
Poor thing.

There Was a Crooked Man

There was a crooked man,
And he walked a crooked mile,
He found a crooked sixpence
Against a crooked stile;
He bought a crooked cat,
Which caught a crooked mouse,
And they all lived together
In a little crooked house.

There Was an Old Woman

There was an old woman tossed up in a baskct,
Nineteen times as high as the moon;
Oh! whither, old woman? I could not but ask it,
For in her hand she carried a broom.
Old woman, old woman, old woman, quoth I,
Where are you going to up so high?
To sweep the cobwebs out of the sky!
Shall I come with you? Aye, by-and-by.

Lucy Locket Lost Her Pocket

Lucy Locket lost her pocket,
Kitty Fisher found it;
There was not a penny in it,
Only ribbon round it.

The Queen of Hearts

The Queen of Hearts
She made some tarts,
All on a summer's day;
The Knave of Hearts
He stole those tarts,
And took them clean away.

The King of Hearts
Called for the tarts,
And beat the Knave full sore;
The Knave of Hearts
Brought back the tarts,
And vowed he'd steal no more.

There Was an Owl Lived in an Oak

There was an owl lived in an oak,
    Wisky, wasky, weedle;
And every word he ever spoke
    Was Fiddle, faddle, feedle.

A gunner chanced to come that way,
    Wisky, wasky weedle;
Says he I'll shoot you, silly bird.
    Fiddle, faddle, feedle.

I Had a Little Nut Tree

I had a little nut tree,
And nothing would it bear
But a silver nutmeg
And a golden pear.

The King of Spain's daughter
Came to visit me,
And all for the sake
Of my little nut tree.

Tweedle Dum and
Tweedle Dee

Tweedle Dum and Tweedle Dee
Agreed to have a battle,
For Tweedle Dum said Tweedle Dee
Had spoiled his nice new rattle.

Just then flew by a monstrous crow,
As big as a tar-barrel,
Which frightened both the heroes so,
They quite forgot their quarrel.

Humpty Dumpty

Humpty Dumpty sat on a wall,
Humpty Dumpty had a great fall.
All the King's horses,
And all the King's men,
Couldn't put Humpty together again.

Mary, Mary, Quite Contrary

Mary, Mary, quite contrary,
How does your garden grow?
With silver bells and cockle shells,
And pretty maids all in a row.

How Many Miles
to Babylon?

How many miles to Babylon?
Three-score miles and ten.
Can I get there by candle-light?
Yes, and back again.
If your heels are nimble and light,
You may get there by candle-light.

One, Two, Buckle My Shoe

1, 2,
Buckle my shoe;

3, 4,
Knock at the door;

5, 6,
Pick up sticks;

7, 8,
Lay them straight;

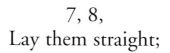

9, 10,
A big fat hen;

11, 12,
Dig and delve;

13, 14,
Maids a-courting;

15, 16,
Maids in the kitchen;

17, 18,
Maids a-waiting;

19, 20,
My plate's empty.

One, Two, Three, Four, Five

One, two, three, four, five,
Once I caught a fish alive,
Six, seven, eight, nine, ten,
Then I let it go again.
Why did you let it go?
Because it bit my finger so.
Which finger did it bite?
This little finger on my right.

Jack Sprat

Jack Sprat could eat no fat,
His wife could eat no lean,
And so between them both, you see,
They licked the platter clean.

Tom, Tom, the Piper's Son

Tom, Tom, the piper's son,
Stole a pig and away he run;
The pig was eat,
And Tom was beat,
And Tom went howling down the street.

There Was an Old Woman
Who Lived in a Shoe

There was an old woman who lived in a shoe,
She had so many children she didn't know what to do;
She gave them some broth without any bread;
Then whipped them all soundly and sent them to bed.

Hickory, Dickory Dock

Hickory, dickory dock,
The mouse ran up the clock.
The clock struck one,
The mouse ran down,
Hickory, dickory dock.

The Man in the Moon

The man in the moon
Came tumbling down,
And asked his way to Norwich;
He went by the south,
And burnt his mouth
With supping cold plum porridge.

Georgie Porgie

Georgie Porgie, pudding and pie,
Kissed the girls and made them cry;
When the boys came out to play,
Georgie Porgie ran away.

To Market, to Market

To market, to market,
To buy a fat pig,
Home again, home again,
Jiggety-jig.
To market, to market,
To buy a fat hog,
Home again, home again,
Jiggety-jog.

Little Tommy Tucker

Little Tommy Tucker
Sings for his supper:
What shall we give him?
White bread and butter.
How shall he cut it
Without e'er a knife?
How will he be married
Without e'er a wife?

One Misty, Moisty Morning

One misty, moisty morning,
When cloudy was the weather,
There I met an old man
All dressed in leather.

All dressed in leather,
With cap under his chin:
How do you do, and how do you do,
And how do you do again?

Little Poll Parrot

Little Poll Parrot
Sat in her garret
Eating toast and tea;
A little brown mouse
Jumped into the house,
And stole it all away.

Dr Foster Went to Gloucester

Dr Foster went to Gloucester
In a shower of rain;
He stepped in a puddle,
Right up to his middle,
And never went there again.

It's Raining, it's Pouring

It's raining, it's pouring
The old man's snoring.
He went to bed,
And bumped his head,
And couldn't get up in the morning.

Rain, Rain, Go Away

Rain, rain, go away,
Come again another day.

Baa, Baa, Black Sheep

Baa, baa, black sheep,
Have you any wool?
Yes, sir, yes, sir,
Three bags full;
One for my master,
And one for my dame,
And one for the little boy
Who lives down the lane.

When I Was a Little Boy

When I was a little boy
I lived by myself,
And all the bread and cheese I had
I laid upon the shelf.

The rats and mice
They led me such a life,
I had to go to London town
And get me a wife.

The streets were so broad
And the lanes were so narrow,
I had to bring my wife home
In a wheelbarrow.

The wheelbarrow broke
And my wife took a fall,
Farewell wheelbarrow,
Little wife and all.

The Cat Came Fiddling

The cat came fiddling out of the barn,
With a pair of bag-pipes under her arm;
She could sing nothing but, Fiddle cum fee,
The mouse has married the bumble-bee.
Pipe, cat; dance, mouse;
We'll have a wedding at our good house.

If All the Seas Were One Sea

If all the seas were one sea,
What a **great** sea that would be!
If all the trees were one tree,
What a **great** tree that would be!
If all the axes were one axe,
What a **great** axe that would be!
And if all the men were one man,
What a **great** man that would be!
And if the **great** man took the **great** axe,
And cut down the **great** tree,
And let it fall into the **great** sea,
What a splish-splash that would be!

Little Tommy Tittlemouse

Little Tommy Tittlemouse
Lived in a little house;
He caught fishes
In other men's ditches.

Round and Round the Garden

Round and round the garden,
Like a teddy bear.
One step, two steps,
And tickle you under there!

Three Blind Mice

Three blind mice, see how they run!
They all ran after the farmer's wife,
Who cut off their tails with a carving knife,
Did you ever see such a thing in your life,
As three blind mice?

Yankee Doodle Came to Town

Yankee Doodle came to town,
Riding on a pony;
He stuck a feather in his cap
And called it macaroni.

The Galloping Major

Bumpety, bumpety, bumpety, bump,
As though I was riding my charger,
Bumpety, bumpety, bumpety, bump,
Just like an Indian rajah.

All the girls declare,
That I'm a gay old stager,
Hey, hey, clear the way!
Here comes the galloping major.

Mary Had a Little Lamb

Mary had a little lamb,
Its fleece was white as snow;
And everywhere that Mary went
The lamb was sure to go.

It followed her to school one day,
This was against the rule;
It made the children laugh and play
To see a lamb at school.

Ring-a-Ring O'Roses

Ring-a-ring o'roses,
A pocket full of posies,
A-tishoo! A-tishoo!
We all fall down.

The cows are in the meadow
Eating buttercups,
A-tishoo! A-tishoo!
We all get up.

Sally Go Round the Sun

Sally go round the sun,
Sally go round the moon,
Sally go round the chimney pots
On a Saturday afternoon.

Hickety, Pickety, My Black Hen

Hickety, pickety, my black hen,
She lays eggs for gentlemen;
Gentlemen come every day
To see what my black hen doth lay.
Sometimes nine and sometimes ten,
Hickety, pickety, my black hen.

Little Jumping Joan

Here am I,
Little Jumping Joan;
When nobody's with me
I'm all alone.

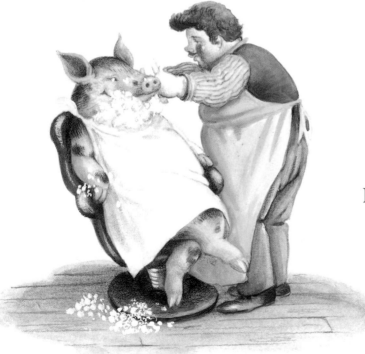

Barber, Barber Shave a Pig

Barber, barber shave a pig,
How many hairs will make a wig?
Four and twenty, that's enough,
Give the barber a pinch of snuff.

Christmas Is a-Coming

Christmas is a-coming,
The geese are getting fat,
Please to put a penny
In the old man's hat.
If you haven't got a penny,
A ha'penny will do;
If you haven't got a ha'penny,
Then God bless you.

Jack Be Nimble

Jack be nimble,
Jack be quick,
Jack jump over
The candlestick.

Daffy-Down-Dilly

Daffy-Down-Dilly
is new come to town,
With a yellow petticoat,
and a green gown.

Old Mother Goose

Old Mother Goose

Old Mother Goose,
When she wanted to wander,
Would ride through the air
On a very fine gander.

Mother Goose had a house,
'Twas built in a wood,
Where an owl at the door
As sentinel stood.

She had a son Jack,
A plain looking lad,
He was not very good,
Nor yet very bad.

She sent him to market,
A live goose he bought;
See, Mother, says he,
I have not been for nought.

Jack's goose and her gander
Grew very fond;
They'd both eat together,
Or swim in the pond.

Jack found one morning,
As I have been told,
His goose had laid him
An egg of pure gold.

Jack ran to his mother
The news for to tell,
She called him a good boy,
And said it was well.

Jack sold his egg
To a merchant untrue,
Who cheated him out of
Half of his due.

Then Jack went a-courting
A lady so gay,
As fair as the lily,
And as sweet as the May.

The merchant and squire
Soon came back,
And began to belabour
The sides of poor Jack.

Then old Mother Goose
That instant came in,
And turned her son Jack
Into famed Harlequin.

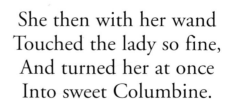

She then with her wand
Touched the lady so fine,
And turned her at once
Into sweet Columbine.

The gold egg in the sea
Was thrown away then,
When an odd fish brought her
The egg back again.

The merchant then vowed
The goose he would kill,
Resolving at once
His pockets to fill.

Jack's mother came in,
And caught the goose soon,
And mounting its back,
Flew up to the moon.

Gregory Griggs, Gregory Griggs

Gregory Griggs, Gregory Griggs,
Had twenty-seven different wigs.
He wore them up, he wore them down,
To please the people of the town;
He wore them east, he wore them west,
But he never could tell which he loved best.

As I Was Going to St. Ives

As I was going to St. Ives,
I met a man with seven wives,
Each wife had seven sacks,
Each sack had seven cats,
Each cat had seven kits:
Kits, cats, sacks, and wives,
How many were going to St. Ives?

I Saw a Ship a-Sailing

I saw a ship a-sailing,
A-sailing on the sea,
And oh, but it was laden
With pretty things for thee!

There were comfits in the cabin,
And apples in the hold;
The sails were made of silk,
The masts were all of gold.

The four-and-twenty sailors,
That stood between the decks,
Were four-and-twenty white mice
With chains around their necks.

The captain was a duck
With a packet on his back,
And when the ship began to move
The captain said Quack! Quack!

Little Jack Horner

Little Jack Horner
Sat in a corner,
Eating a Christmas pie;
He put in his thumb,
And pulled out a plum,
And said, What a good boy am I!

Elizabeth, Elspeth, Betsy and Bess

Elizabeth, Elspeth, Betsy and Bess,
They all went together to seek a bird's nest;
They found a bird's nest with five eggs in,
They all took one, and left four in.

Old King Cole

Old King Cole
Was a merry old soul,
And a merry old soul was he;
He called for his pipe,
And he called for his bowl,
And he called for his fiddlers three.

Every fiddler had a fiddle,
And a very fine fiddle had he;
Oh! There's none so rare
As can compare
With King Cole and his fiddlers three.

Down With the Lamb

Down with the lamb,
Up with the lark.
Go to bed children
Before it gets dark.

Wee Willie Winkie

Wee Willie Winkie runs through the town,
Upstairs and downstairs in his night gown,
Rapping at the window, calling through the lock,
Are the children all in bed, it's now eight o'clock.

Old Mother Slipper Slopper

Old Mother Slipper Slopper jumped out of bed,
And out of the window she popped her head:
Oh! John, John, John, the grey goose is gone,
And the fox is off to his den O!
Den O! Den O!
Oh! John, John, John, the grey goose is gone,
And the fox is off to his den O!

Little Bo-Peep

Little Bo-Peep has lost her sheep,
And doesn't know where to find them;
Leave them alone and they'll come home,
Bringing their tails behind them.

Little Bo-Peep fell fast asleep,
And dreamt she heard them bleating;
But when she awoke, she found it a joke,
For they were still a-fleeting.

Then up she took her little crook,
Determined for to find them;
She found them indeed, but it made her heart bleed,
For they'd left their tails behind them.

It happened one day, as Bo-Peep did stray
Into a meadow hard by,
She espied their tails side by side,
All hung on a tree to dry.

She heaved a sigh, and wiped her eye,
And over the hillocks went rambling,
And tried what she could, as a shepherdess should,
To tack again each to its lambkin.

Little Polly Flinders

Little Polly Flinders
Sat among the cinders,
Warming her pretty little toes;
Her mother came and caught her,
And smacked her little daughter
For spoiling her nice new clothes.

Ladybird, Ladybird

Ladybird, ladybird,
Fly away home,
Your house is on fire
And your children are gone;
All except one
And that's little Ann
And she has crept under
The warming pan.

Sing a Song of Sixpence

Sing a song of sixpence,
A pocket full of rye;
Four and twenty blackbirds,
Baked in a pie.

When the pie was opened,
The birds began to sing;
Was not that a dainty dish,
To set before the king?

The king was in his counting-house
Counting out his money;
The queen was in the parlour,
Eating bread and honey.

The maid was in the garden,
Hanging out the clothes,
When down came a blackbird
And pecked off her nose.

Old Mother Twitchett Has But One Eye

Old Mother Twitchett has but one eye,
And a long tail which she can let fly,
And every time she goes over a gap,
She leaves a bit of her tail in a trap.

Black Am I and Much Admired

Black am I and much admired,
Men seek for me until they're tired;
When they find me, break my head,
And take me from my resting bed.

Little Nancy Etticoat

Little Nancy Etticoat,
Has a white petticoat,
And a red nose;
The longer she stands
The shorter she grows.

I Love Little Pussy

I love little pussy,
Her coat is so warm,
And if I don't hurt her
She'll do me no harm.
So I'll not pull her tail,
Nor drive her away,
But Pussy and I
Very gently will play.
She'll sit by my side,
And I'll give her some food;
And pussy will love me
Because I am good.

Old Mother Hubbard

Old Mother Hubbard
Went to the cupboard,
To fetch her poor dog a bone;
But when she got there
The cupboard was bare
And so her poor dog had none.

She went to the baker's
To buy him some bread;
But when she came back
The poor dog was dead.

She went to the joiner's
To buy him a coffin;
But when she came back
The poor dog was laughing.

She took a clean dish
To get him some tripe;
But when she came back
He was smoking a pipe.

She went to the fishmonger's
To buy him some fish;
But when she came back
He was licking the dish.

She went to the ale house
To get him some beer;
But when she came back
The dog sat in a chair.

She went to the tavern
For white wine and red;
But when she came back
The dog stood on his head.

She went to the hatter's
To buy him a hat;
But when she came back
He was feeding the cat.

She went to the barber's
To buy him a wig;
But when she came back
He was dancing a jig.

She went to the fruiterer's
To buy him some fruit;
But when she came back
He was playing the flute.

She went to the tailor's
To buy him a coat;
But when she came back
He was riding a goat.

She went to the cobbler's
To buy him some shoes;
But when she came back
He was reading the news.

She went to the seamstress
To buy him some linen;
But when she came back
The dog was a-spinning.

She went to the hosier's
To buy him some hose;
But when she came back
He was dressed in his clothes.

The dame made a curtsey,
The dog made a bow;
The dame said, Your servant,
The dog said, Bow-wow.

Four Stiff-Standers

Four stiff-standers,
Four dilly-danders,
Two lookers,
Two crookers,
And a wig-wag.

Two Little Dicky Birds

Two little dicky birds,
Sitting on the wall:
One named Peter,
One named Paul!
Fly away Peter!
Fly away Paul!
Come back Peter!
Come back Paul!

Polly Put the Kettle On

Polly put the kettle on,
Polly put the kettle on,
Polly put the kettle on,
We'll all have tea.

Sukey take it off again,
Sukey take it off again,
Sukey take it off again,
They've all gone away.

Jack and Jill

Jack and Jill
Went up the hill,
To fetch a pail of water;
Jack fell down,
And broke his crown,
And Jill came tumbling after.

Then up Jack got,
And home he trot,
As fast as he could caper;
And went to bed,
To mend his head,
With vinegar and brown paper.

Pussy Cat Mole

Pussy cat Mole jumped over a coal
And in her best petticoat burnt a great hole.
Poor pussy's weeping, she'll have no more milk
Until her best petticoat's mended with silk.

Matthew, Mark, Luke and John

Matthew, Mark, Luke and John,
Bless the bed that I lie on.
Four corners to my bed,
Four angels round my head;
One to watch and one to pray
And two to bear my soul away.

Round About There

Round about there
Sat a little hare
The bow-wows came and chased him
Right up there!

Bye, Baby Bunting

Bye, baby bunting,
Daddy's gone a-hunting.
Gone to get a rabbit skin
To wrap his baby bunting in.

Ding, Dong, Bell

Ding, dong, bell,
Pussy's in the well.
Who put her in?
Little Johnny Green.
Who pulled her out?
Little Tommy Stout.
What a naughty boy was that
To try to drown poor pussy cat,
Who never did any harm,
And killed the mice in his father's barn.

Dance to Your Daddy

Dance to your daddy,
My little babby,
Dance to your daddy,
My little lamb.

You shall have a fishy
On a little dishy,
You shall have a fishy
When the boat comes in.

Goosey, Goosey Gander

Goosey, goosey gander,
Whither shall I wander?
Upstairs and downstairs
And in my lady's chamber.
There I met an old man
Who would not say his prayers,
So I took him by the left leg
And threw him down the stairs.

There Was a Little Girl

There was a little girl, and she had a little curl
Right in the middle of her forehead;
When she was good she was very, very good,
But when she was bad she was horrid.

This Little Piggy Went to Market

This little piggy went to market,

This little piggy stayed at home,

This little piggy ate roast beef,

This little piggy had none,

And this little piggy went,
Wee-wee-wee-wee,
All the way home.

Blue Bell

I had a little dog, and his name was Blue Bell,
I gave him some work, and he did it very well;
I sent him upstairs to pick up a pin,
He stepped in a coal-scuttle up to his chin;
I sent him to the garden to pick some sage,
He tumbled down and fell in a rage;
I sent him to the cellar to draw a pot of beer,
He came up again and said there was none there.

A Frog He
Would a-Wooing Go

A Frog He Would a-Wooing Go

A frog he would a-wooing go,
Heigh ho! says Rowley,
A frog he would a-wooing go,
Whether his mother would let him or no.
With a rowley, powley, gammon and spinach,
Heigh ho! says Anthony Rowley.

So off he set with his opera hat,
Heigh ho! says Rowley,
So off he set with his opera hat,
And on the road he met with a rat.
With a rowley, powley, gammon and spinach,
Heigh ho! says Anthony Rowley.

Pray, Mr. Rat, will you go with me?
Heigh ho! says Rowley,
Pray, Mr. Rat will you go with me,
Kind Mrs. Mousey for to see?
With a rowley, powley, gammon and spinach,
Heigh ho! says Anthony Rowley.

They came to the door of Mousey's hall,
Heigh ho! says Rowley,
They gave a loud knock, and they gave a loud call.
With a rowley, powley, gammon and spinach,
Heigh ho! says Anthony Rowley.

Pray, Mrs. Mouse, are you within?
Heigh ho! says Rowley,
Oh yes, kind sirs, I'm sitting to spin.
With a rowley, powley, gammon and spinach,
Heigh ho! says Anthony Rowley.

Pray, Mrs. Mouse, will you give us some beer?
Heigh ho! says Rowley,
For Froggy and I are fond of good cheer.
With a rowley, powley, gammon and spinach,
Heigh ho! says Anthony Rowley.

Pray, Mr. Frog, will you give us a song?
Heigh ho! says Rowley,
Let it be something that's not very long.
With a rowley, powley, gammon and spinach,
Heigh ho! says Anthony Rowley.

Indeed, Mrs. Mouse, replied Mr. Frog,
Heigh ho! says Rowley,
A cold has made me as hoarse as a dog.
With a rowley, powley, gammon and spinach,
Heigh ho! says Anthony Rowley.

Since you have a cold, Mr. Frog, Mousey said,
Heigh ho! says Rowley,
I'll sing you a song that I have just made.
With a rowley, powley, gammon and spinach,
Heigh ho! says Anthony Rowley.

But while they were all a-merry-making,
Heigh ho! says Rowley,
A cat and her kittens came tumbling in.
With a rowley, powley, gammon and spinach,
Heigh ho! says Anthony Rowley.

The cat seized the rat by the crown,
Heigh ho! says Rowley,
The kittens they pulled the little mouse down.
With a rowley, powley, gammon and spinach,
Heigh ho! says Anthony Rowley.

This put Mr. Frog in a terrible fright,
Heigh ho! says Rowley,
He took up his hat and he wished them Good-night.
With a rowley, powley, gammon and spinach,
Heigh ho! says Anthony Rowley.

But as Froggy was crossing over a brook,
Heigh ho! says Rowley,
A lily-white duck came and gobbled him up.
With a rowley, powley, gammon and spinach,
Heigh ho! says Anthony Rowley.

So there was an end of one, two, three,
Heigh ho! says Rowley,
The rat and the mouse and the little Frog-ee
With a rowley, powley, gammon and spinach,
Heigh ho! says Anthony Rowley.

Molly, My Sister
and I Fell Out

Molly, my sister and I fell out,
And what do you think it was all about?
She loved coffee and I loved tea,
And that was the reason we couldn't agree.

Cock-a-Doodle-Doo

Cock-a-doodle-doo!
My dame has lost her shoe,
My master's lost his fiddling stick,
And doesn't know what to do.

Twinkle, Twinkle Little Star

Twinkle, twinkle little star,
How I wonder what you are,
Up above the world so high,
Like a diamond in the sky.

Star Light, Star Bright

Star light, star bright,
First star I see tonight,
I wish I may, I wish I might,
Have the wish I wish tonight.

I See the Moon

I see the moon,
And the moon sees me;
God bless the moon,
And God bless me.

Boys and Girls Come Out to Play

Boys and girls come out to play,
The moon is shining bright as day.
Leave your supper and leave your sleep,
And join your playfellows in the street.
Come with a whoop and come with a call,
Come with a good will or not at all.
Up the ladder and down the wall,
A half-penny loaf will serve us all;
You find the milk, and I'll find the flour,
And we'll have a pudding in half an hour.

Afterword

There can be few activities that provide a very young child with a greater feeling of security than being soothed to sleep with a lullaby; few can bring greater enjoyment than sitting on a parent's lap, the centre of the universe, being treated to some tickling or toe-tweaking game or rumbustious knee-ride. The verses that traditionally accompany this play are the foundations of the nursery rhyme repertoire and the child will remember them the whole of his or her life. The essence of these first nursery verses is simplicity. Whether spoken or sung, their uncomplicated rhyme and robust rhythms ensure they are fun to repeat and always pleasing to the ear. And there can be no ears more receptive than those of a child, nor audience more eager for an encore.

As the child grows, he or she gains a huge store of juvenile songs, riddles and proverbs, counting and alphabet rhymes on which to draw. Verses to accompany baby games make way for those that accompany playground games. Jingles move aside for the ballad. The simple nonsense verse gives way to the complicated accumulative rhyme. From the first cradle song to the last tongue twister, the nursery rhyme covers it all.

While beloved by children, many of our older rhymes were not composed specifically with them in mind. They were gleaned from a myriad of sources: from poems, chapbooks, broad sheets and pamphlets. Some are the remnants of long-forgotten folk songs and ballads, others are snippets from the stage and snatches from the mummers' plays. Still others had their first telling in a more distinctly adult world of the tavern and worse, their meanings and origins obscured by subsequent adaption for a new juvenile audience.

As these early rhymes were rarely written down, they relied on word of mouth for their spread. Handed down from one generation to the next in this manner many versions have evolved. None is incorrect and all are interesting. This lack of standardisation has conferred upon our nursery rhymes variety and a vitality without which some might have become stale.

Just how ancient some of these verses are we will probably never know. As they relied totally on oral transmission for their perpetuation, references to them are scarce, if they exist at all. This makes accurate dating impossible. But we know that many do have long ancestry. The earliest known record of "*Cock-a-doodle-doo*" for instance, appears in 1606 when it is mentioned in connection with a gruesome crime. It was said to have been the first utterance from a child whose tongue had been cut out to prevent her revealing the identity of her brother's murderers. But versions of "*Cock-a-doodle-doo*" may have been around for generations prior to this first mention.

Throughout the eighteenth century, a number of small volumes of verse deemed suitable for children began to circulate. Some were made up of traditional verses and others contained fresh works, specially penned for the nursery. Word of mouth was no longer the only means by which the rhymes were handed down. Enthusiasm for these publications grew and brought with it a surge of new composition and interest in the subject. By the end of the nineteenth century, the nursery anthology as we know it today had appeared.

Over the years, attempts have been made to establish significance to verses whose meanings have otherwise become lost to us. Some have been very far-fetched indeed and never gained acceptance, while others, equally without foundation, have been taken as truth.

It is widely accepted that "*A ring, a ring o'roses*" refers to the dreadful effects of the Great Plague. The "ring o'roses" was the rash associated with the disease; the "pocket full of posies" the nosegay carried to ward off contagion; "A-tishoo! A-tishoo!" the sneezing that heralded the victim's demise, and "We all fall down" the inevitable end. All of which sounds very plausible if it were not for the fact that the first recorded versions of the rhyme do not appear till the late nineteenth century and make no mention whatever of sneezing or falling down.

Inventive efforts have also been made to pin down the identities of various nursery rhyme characters. One such example involves *Old Mother Goose* herself.

An article published in the mid-nineteenth century claimed that an American matron, one Elizabeth Goose, born in Boston, in 1665, was the primary source of many of the rhymes appearing in the nursery collections of the eighteenth century. She was said to have been a woman with a prodigious memory for the songs and ditties of her childhood and to which she in turn treated her many children and grandchildren. Eventually her son-in-law set down her recitations and published them in a volume entitled "Mother Goose's Melodies for Children".

Unfortunately, it appears that the story was a fabrication. "Mother Goose" was in fact already a figure well known in European folklore. She was the guardian of the fairy tale and it is not surprising that her name should have become linked to the nursery rhyme as well.

The modern Mother Goose collection makes a very wide range of nursery rhymes available to our children. It can incorporate new verses as they occur and at the same time protect those that are less well known from extinction.

But what has become of the "oral tradition" itself? Has it died? Far from it. It is alive and well. The proof lies in the number of rhymes that we carry in our heads without ever having made an effort to learn them. They were just absorbed, along with the language itself at our mother's knee. When we in turn repeat them to our own children, we ensure their survival. The oral tradition is one in which we all have a part to play. It is our guarantee that the nursery rhyme will live as long as there are children to hear it.

For further information on nursery rhymes, the reader can do no better than refer to The Oxford Dictionary of Nursery Rhymes, Oxford University Press 1997, edited by Iona and Peter Opie whose scholarship has made the history of this fascinating subject accessible to all.